I WITNESSED
THE INDIAN OCEAN TSUNAMI

THE INDIAN OCEAN TSUNAMI

JOHN SMITH-SREEN

JUGGERNAUT BOOKS
C-I-128, First Floor, Sangam Vihar, Near Holi Chowk,
New Delhi 110080, India

First published by Juggernaut Books 2025

Copyright © John Smith-Sreen 2025

10 9 8 7 6 5 4 3 2 1

P-ISBN: 9789353452988
E-ISBN: 9789353453718

The views and opinions expressed in this book are the author's own. The facts contained herein were reported to be true as on the date of publication by the author to the publishers of the book, and the publishers are not in any way liable for their accuracy or veracity.

This book contains descriptions of real-life disasters and loss of life. Reader discretion is advised.

The international boundaries on the maps of India are neither purported to be correct nor authentic by Survey of India directives.

All rights reserved. No part of this publication may be reproduced, transmitted or stored in a retrieval system in any form or by any means without the written permission of the publisher.

Typeset in Futura Std by R. Ajith Kumar, Noida

Printed at Thomson Press India Ltd

To Poonam who helped me weather the storms and to Sasha, Tanya and Joshua who inspired me to write about them.

CONTENTS

1. Rocks — 1
2. Checking In and Checking Out — 13
3. The Earthquake and the Wave — 47
4. Tsunami Madness — 53
5. The Blue Boat — 65
6. The Importance of Trees — 73
7. View from the Veranda — 81
8. Rescue — 93
9. Reunion and Recovery — 99
10. Let's Go Home — 113

Postscript: A Report on Tsunamis — 119

1
ROCKS

'Look at this one, Tara!' Arun shouts, holding up a small brown rock. 'It's got a seashell in it!'

He's way too excited. Again.

'I spent hours in the garden digging these up,' he says, thrusting the rock at her face. 'See, see!'

Tara sighs inwardly. She loves her brother – but rocks? Not her thing. Still, she takes the rock and pretends to care.

'Oooh. Nice,' she says, giving him a quick smile and handing it back.

That's all the encouragement Arun needs.

'Check this one out! It's mica. Looks like *chandni*, right?'

Tara nods. 'Pretty,' she says politely, already inching towards the door.

But Arun blocks her path. 'Wait! I have more. The best ones are still in the box –'

'I think Papa said something about a family caucus!' Tara blurts, slipping past him. 'I'm going to find Sunil!'

When their parents say 'family caucus', it usually means something important – like where they're going for vacation. Tara races down the hall.

She finds Sunil with his nose in a book, as usual. He glances up. 'What's up?'

'Arun's showing me his rock collection. Again.'

Sunil snorts. 'Bet that was thrilling.'

They both giggle. They love Arun – but he *really* gets into things. Fossils, stamps, ancient coins, random insects. And, of course, rocks.

'What are you reading?' Tara asks.

'*A History of Rocks*,' Sunil deadpans.

That sends them into another round of laughter as they tumble down the stairs together.

In the living room, the family caucus is already underway.

'I don't *want* to go to the beach,' Arun complains. 'The mountains are better. What even *is* this Tamil Nadu place?'

He crosses his arms. 'Why do we have to go? I want to spend Christmas *here*, in our house! I want to stay in Sikkim!'

The Sonis *always* celebrate Christmas. Mr Soni's mom – Dadi – was Christian, and even though she wasn't big on church, she loved the holiday. Mr Soni kept the tradition going, and the kids definitely didn't mind. Christmas at home meant cake, songs and a twinkly tree. Sunil always says they're happy to celebrate *all* holidays – Hindu, Muslim, Christian, Sikh, Jain – India has plenty!

Mr Soni explains the plan. 'We *live* in the mountains right now,' he says, 'so vacation should be something different. Tamil Nadu has temples, beaches, palm trees. It's a whole new world.'

Arun scowls. Then shrugs. 'Okay, fine. Beach it is.'

Suddenly, the room explodes with cheers.

'The beach! The beach! The beach!'

They're headed to a place called Mahabalipuram. The name is so long and musical, the kids break it into chunks just to say it.

'MA-HA-BA-LI-PUR-AM!'

Soon they're dancing around the house, chanting the name like it's a song.

Sunil looks it up online. 'It's a UNESCO World Heritage Site,' he announces. 'There's an ancient temple right by the sea. The views are amazing. And guess what?'

He scrolls through photos. 'Our hotel has a huge balcony facing the ocean!'

As departure day gets closer, excitement buzzes through the house.

Arun's suitcase is already packed and sitting by his door.

Tara is still deciding which outfit matches which day.

Sunil is buried in his guidebook, making a list of all the places to visit: the Shore Temple, the Five Rathas … and Krishna's Butterball.

'Arun,' he says one evening, 'you'll like this.'

Arun glances up. 'Yeah?'

'Krishna's Butterball is a rock.'

Arun perks up. 'Go on …'

Sunil grins. 'A *giant* rock. Balanced perfectly on a slope. Legend says Lord Krishna placed it there with just one finger.'

He shows him a photo – an enormous boulder, resting like magic at the top of a hill. A tiny man stands beside it, looking like an ant.

'Cool,' Arun whispers.

Tara's eyes go wide. 'What if it rolls down?' she says nervously.

Sunil laughs. 'That's the fun part!'

And with that, Mahabalipuram starts to sound like the best idea ever.

2
CHECKING IN AND CHECKING OUT

The flight to Chennai is long, but uneventful – just enough turbulence to keep it interesting, and just enough snacks to keep everyone content. As soon as the wheels touch down, the Soni family springs into action. The children keep a sharp eye on one particular suitcase – the one with the Christmas presents – as they wait at the baggage carousel.

Outside the airport, it doesn't take long to spot their ride. A cheerful young man in a plaid shirt and a towel-like cloth wrapped around his waist stands holding a sign that reads 'Soni'.

'Welacome,' he says, stretching the greeting into three syllables.

The kids burst into grins. 'Welacome! Welacome!' they echo under their breath, giggling as they follow their parents through the crowd.

With the luggage strapped securely to the roof of the car and the kids squashed happily in the back seat, the family begins their journey down the scenic East Coast Road towards Mahabalipuram. Their driver chats as he drives, telling them that the town is famous for its sandy beaches and its ancient, sea-battered stone temples — one of the oldest in India. Though centuries of salt spray and monsoon storms have done their best, the temple still stands proudly, facing the wide blue sweep of the Indian Ocean.

Their hotel is something out of a postcard — grassy lawns stretched towards a low red-brick wall, beyond which lies golden sand and glittering blue sea. From the bluff a short way down the beach, the famous stone temple rises from the coast like something half-remembered from a dream.

'Mahabalipuram! Mahabalipuram!' the children shout with delight.

'Race you!' cries Arun, already kicking off his shoes.

'Check in first!' their mother calls behind them.

But Arun hollers back, 'We're checking out!' and all three kids tear off down the sand.

It turns out the temple is farther than it looks. Soon they are puffing, feet dragging through the soft sand, though the boys try to look cool. Tara's legs are shorter, but she pumps them fiercely, determined to keep up.

Just before the temple, a chain-link and barbed-wire fence stretches all the way into the ocean. The posts lean at odd angles, some pulled loose from the concrete by wind or waves.

The kids find a gap in seconds.

'Careful,' warns Sunil. 'That stuff can give you tetanus. You do *not* want a tetanus shot.'

Tara shivers. She doesn't know exactly what tetanus is, but she *definitely* doesn't want a shot. Her father has to wrestle her like a wild cat every time she needs one. So, she tiptoes through the gap with maximum caution.

And then – they are in.

The temple looms before them. Stone lions, eroded by centuries of salt and sand, guard the staircase. Some are just headless lumps now, but others still have their faces – proud, fierce and magnificent.

'Mama said this thing is *thousands* of years old,' Arun whispers.

'Really?' Tara gasps. 'You mean like … DINOSAUR old?!'

'Dinosaurs!' shout Arun and Sunil in unison.

'No, wait' Sunil says patiently. 'Dinosaurs were millions of years ago. But this is still *really* old.'

'Idiot,' adds Arun, just for good measure.

Tara ignores him. She is too mesmerized. The stairs are massive. The air is still and thick with

the smell of stone and salt. As they climb, they whisper again, not because they have to – but because the place *asks* for it.

They duck into alcoves, scramble over carved rocks and marvel at half-erased deities. One goddess catches Tara's eye. Her face, unlike most of the others, is still whole – smiling gently in the golden light.

'She's beautiful,' Tara breathes. 'Why did *she* keep her face?'

'Harder rock,' Arun says, like an expert.

'Or maybe she's on the sheltered side,' offers Sunil.

Tara nods thoughtfully, still gazing.

'Hey guys! Come look at this!' Arun calls from a dark doorway.

They step inside – and stop short. It is cold, musty and deeply shadowed.

'Ugh. What's that smell?' Tara groans.

'Shh. Listen,' Arun whispers.

High above, in the shadows near the ceiling, comes a faint squeaking.

As their eyes adjust, they see it. The ceiling is *moving*.

'It's alive!' Arun shouts.

'It's *swarming*,' says Sunil.

'It's *disgusting*,' moans Tara.

Hundreds of bats cling upside down to the ceiling, twitching and rustling. Arun grins, picks up a pebble and lobs it into the air.

'No–!' Sunil begins, but it is too late.

Chaos. Wings. Screeches. A living cloud of bats explodes into the air, zooming madly in every direction. Tara screams. All three kids bolt out into the sun, shrieking and laughing.

'You idiot!' Sunil yells, punching his brother's shoulder.

'Rats with wings!' Arun cackles.

Tara doesn't laugh. She'd been really scared. Tears prick at her eyes, but she blinks them

away. Sunil notices and puts an arm around her. She leans into him, comforted.

'Let's head back before Arun gets us arrested,' he says with a grin.

And they do, laughing all the way down the beach, towards their parents and the warm Christmas Eve that awaits them.

That evening, the hotel restaurant serves a feast – fluffy white idlis, crisp golden dosas and steaming bowls of spicy sambar. The children prefer the dosas, especially the plain ones, though their parents opt for the stuffed version with spiced potatoes. They dip pieces into the lentil-rich curry and add a dollop of cool coconut chutney.

'Not as good as tandoori chicken,' says Arun, dramatically. 'But it'll do.'

Their father raises an eyebrow. 'You never have tandoori chicken on Christmas Eve,' he says. 'At home, we always have macaroni and cheese with shrimp curry.'

'Right,' says Sunil, grinning. 'Macaroni and cheese because you hated shrimp as kids.'

'And your grandparents didn't want to change their menu,' adds their mother.

'Exactly,' says their father. 'Tradition.'

Later, curled up in their room, the children listen as their dad reads *'Twas the Night Before Christmas.* But instead of sugarplums, their dreams that night are full of wind-worn stone lions and clouds of swirling bats.

Christmas morning arrives with sunshine and excitement. Tara is the first to leap out of bed.

'Let's go! Let's go!' she whispers urgently. 'Did Santa *come*?'

He had.

Somehow, a potted palm has appeared in the room, and beneath it, gleaming, ribbon-wrapped presents. Arun, as the eldest, is given the honour of distributing them slowly, while the others bounce on their heels.

After breakfast – fluffy *appams*, sweet *pongal* and more dosas – they tumble out onto the lawn. The morning is golden and perfect. The grass is soft, bordered by a low brick seawall. Bright bougainvillea and hibiscus blooms explode in colour along the edge. A set of stone steps leads down to the sea.

The parents sit sipping chai in the sun, while the children make for the waves.

Just beyond the resort, a line of fishing boats lies pulled up on the sand. The children wander over, curious. Two boys sit in the shade of a boat.

'Hello,' Tara says brightly.

'Hello,' they reply.

'What are you doing?'

'Waiting for our fathers,' one of them answers. 'They're out fishing. If it's a good catch, we help our mothers take it to market.'

Tara studies the boys – thin, barefoot, sun-darkened. Their lives seem shaped by the sea, but not in the carefree way hers is.

'Where do you live?' she asks.

'Just over the rise,' one of them says, pointing towards a small cluster of shacks made of tin, tarp and driftwood.

'We're staying in that hotel,' Tara says. 'It's really nice.'

'It looks nice,' one boy says softly. 'We've never been.'

'But it's so close!' Tara cries. 'You should visit!'

The boys exchange a look and shrug. Even at their young age, they know better. They'd never be let in.

Suddenly, one of them shouts, 'They're coming!'

A long blue boat surges through the surf. The fishermen shout and laugh as they leap into the water, guiding the boat to shore. Its hull is heavy with wriggling silver fish.

'Whoa! That's got to be a million!' exclaims Arun.

Sunil leans closer. 'Sea bass, red snapper … and look! A barracuda.'

He explains how overfishing, pollution and climate change are hurting the marine ecosystem around Mahabalipuram.

'So … we're killing the fish?' Tara asks, eyes wide.

'Not us exactly,' says Sunil. 'Big fishing companies are the real problem. These guys? Their catch is tiny in comparison.'

More boats arrive. Women hurry to collect fish, children run laughing, and teams of men work together to drag the boats safely ashore – some using logs, others using ropes and wooden yokes.

'Do you ever catch turtles?' Tara asks.

'Sometimes,' one boy admits. 'But we're supposed to let them go.'

'*Supposed to,*' Sunil repeats carefully.

The boys don't reply. Sometimes the turtles die in the nets. Sometimes they wash ashore.

It is a fact of life. One that Tara, thankfully, doesn't yet know.

They speak more – about school, and how the boys don't go anymore. How they help with boats and nets instead. How even free school isn't really free if you have to buy books and uniforms.

'If we don't catch fish,' one boy says, 'we don't eat.'

The three Soni children are quiet. The difference between their lives and those of the boys is suddenly very clear.

'I'm sorry,' Tara whispers.

And she means it.

Their two new friends simply shrug, wave goodbye and dash off to help unload the morning's catch. It has been a good haul. Most of the fish will be sold to middlemen at the market, but a few lucky ones will end up bubbling away in a spicy curry at home. Sunil had explained earlier that not every day was this fortunate. Sometimes, the nets came back nearly empty, and their families had little to eat or sell.

'Come on, you two,' Arun says eagerly. 'I want to see the rock.'

'What rock?' Sunil asks, feigning innocence.

Arun rolls his eyes. 'You know … Krishna's Butterball!'

So, the trio hails a rickshaw from the hotel and rides off towards the famous giant boulder resting precariously on a hillside in Mahabalipuram. Their driver is a cheerful man who likes to talk. He drives a sleek, new electric autorickshaw made by Bajaj. The kids are fascinated – it is their first time in an electric vehicle.

'Why electric?' Sunil asks, eyebrows raised. 'Aren't most rickshaws switching to CNG now?'

'My boss insisted,' the driver says with a grin. 'He says electric is the future, and we should be ahead of the curve.'

'But isn't charging a hassle?' Sunil asks, leaning forward. 'What kind of range do you get?'

'Oh, I can drive all over Mahabalipuram in a day on one charge,' the driver replies. 'But I don't have electricity at home – none of my neighbours do either. We're mostly rickshaw drivers, and the rest are fisherfolk. Good people. We look out for each other. They give us fish

sometimes, and we give them free rides when we can.'

'Then how do you charge it?' Sunil presses, clearly intrigued.

'Easy,' says the driver with a chuckle. 'I park at my boss's house after work and plug it in overnight. Next morning, it's ready to go. And no fuel bills – it's much cheaper,' he adds with a wink.

Sunil nods, lost in thought. He'd read that India is poised to become a global leader in electric vehicles, though the technology is still young. He is quietly impressed that even rickshaw drivers in Tamil Nadu are part of that change. Tara claps her hands in delight. 'I love it! No stinky fumes – and it's so quiet.'

The driver agrees with a laugh as they pull up in front of Krishna's Butterball. The three children step out and stare, awestruck, at the enormous rock. It is somehow balancing at an impossible angle, high above the town.

'Now that's a rock,' says Arun, eyes wide with wonder.

Sunil and Tara nod. None of them have ever seen anything like it – a stone that seems frozen in place by divine mischief.

'Let's just hope there's no earthquake,' Arun jokes. 'Or that butterball will roll for a six!'

Sunil, always ready with a fact, replies, 'Actually, earthquakes are rare in South India. When they do happen in Tamil Nadu, they're usually offshore and pretty mild. You'd feel one at home in Sikkim long before here.'

Later, back at the hotel, the children excitedly share their adventure with their parents. Arun can't stop talking about the rock, while Sunil repeats his reassuring earthquake facts. Tara, smiling shyly, says she hopes they can invite

their new friends from the fishing village to visit the resort.

Her parents exchange soft smiles – ones that hold both affection and a quiet ache – and say yes, that would be lovely.

That night, sun-kissed and tired, the whole family turns in early. None of them can know that the following day will be unlike any other – a day that will shake their world in ways they cannot imagine.

3

THE EARTHQUAKE AND THE WAVE

The kids had no idea that while they were chatting with the fishing boys and marvelling at Krishna's Butterball, something terrifying was happening far away – underneath the sea near the island of Sumatra in Indonesia.

Deep below the ocean floor, the Earth was rumbling. It wasn't a regular kind of shaking. Giant plates of rock were pushing, grinding and suddenly slipping. It was like someone had snapped a giant branch in two. The ground shook with enormous force, creating a massive underwater earthquake.

Nobody on land felt it much. The earthquake's epicentre – its starting point – was way out in

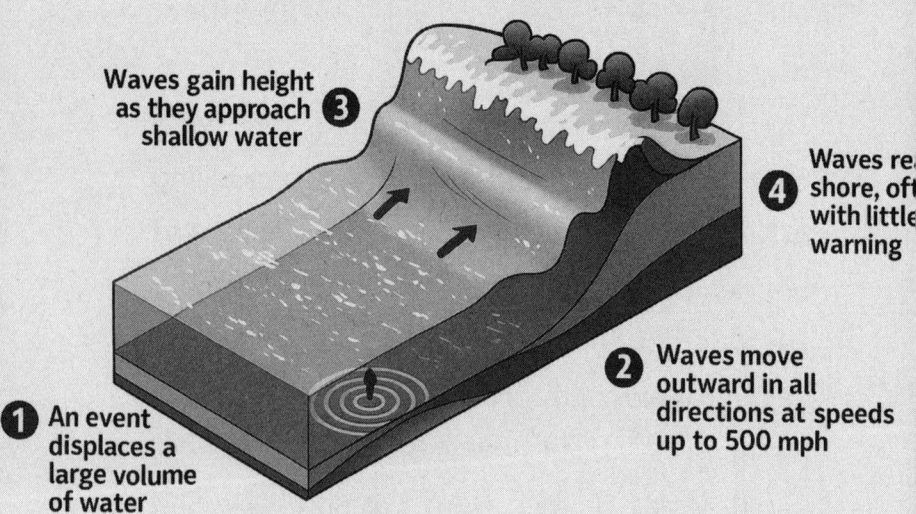

the ocean. So there were no buildings crashing or cracks opening up in the ground. That's why people didn't realize what was coming.

But the ocean did.

Huge waves started forming and crashed into Indonesia. The energy from the earthquake pushed the water in all directions. Out in the deep sea, the waves didn't look like much. But as they raced across the Indian Ocean – heading towards Thailand, Sri Lanka and India – they grew taller and stronger.

What started as a shift in the sea floor would become one of the deadliest tsunamis in history.

And it was heading straight for Mahabalipuram.

4

TSUNAMI MADNESS

Back in their hotel room, the Soni family is waking up on 26 December. Tara sits up in bed, rubbing her eyes. Then comes a sound – shouting from the beach.

Arun runs to the window. 'Whoa! The ocean's gone!'

The rest of the family crowds around. It is true. The water has pulled way, way back from the shore. The beach is now twice as wide as it had been yesterday.

People are running out, laughing and pointing. There are strange little pools everywhere, full of fish and starfish and other sea creatures that

have been left behind. The fishermen's boats are stuck on dry sand.

'Let's go check it out!' Sunil says, already sprinting for the door.

But their father stops him with a firm 'Wait!'

The kids groan. 'You're always worried,' Sunil complains. 'You're like the Fun Police!'

'Come on, Papa,' says Arun. 'What's the big deal?'

Even Tara chimes in. 'Please? Just a quick look?'

Mr Soni looks out of the window again. Something doesn't feel right. He can't explain it, but his stomach is tight with worry.

'Stay here. I'll go look,' he says, pulling on his shoes.

The kids lean over the porch railing, shouting encouragement.

'Run, Papa!'

'Go, go, go!'

'Fat man on a mission!' Arun teases, making everyone laugh.

Mr Soni walks down to the beach. His feet sink into the wet sand. It is sticky and weird, like walking through soft clay. People are everywhere – picking up crabs, taking photos, laughing. Most are staring down, not up.

That's why they don't see it coming.

But Mr Soni hears it.

A sound like thunder. Like a train coming at full speed. And then – Tara's scream.

'PAPA!'

He spins around. His heart drops.

A giant wave is heading straight for the shore.

'GET OFF THE BEACH!' he shouts at the top of his lungs. Many people look up at him with bewildered faces. He turns and runs, feet fighting the sticky sand. His legs pump hard. He can hear the roar behind him getting louder.

Up the seawall steps.

Across the hotel lawn.

He leaps onto the porch where his family is standing.

'INSIDE!' he yells, shoving the door shut just as —

CRASH!

The wave hits.

The big front window explodes. Glass flies everywhere. Saltwater gushes in like a monster.

Mr Soni grabs Tara and Sunil. Mrs Soni holds onto him tightly. Arun feels himself go under. The water is freezing. Furniture floats by like toys in a bathtub.

Arun pushes up with all his strength and — bang! — his head hits the ceiling.

Wait … the ceiling?

He is floating so high that the ceiling fan is right next to him. He grabs it like a lifeline, dazed. Water is everywhere — rushing, roaring, swirling. Pieces of wrapping paper and his brand-new Christmas shoes zip past.

'ARUN!' his mom screams.

Arun barely has time to react.

The ceiling fan rips out of the ceiling. He flies with it, crashing through the broken window.

Pain slices across his side. He slams into the brick seawall, tries to hold on –

But the wall crumbles.

And then he is gone – swept out to sea.

5

THE BLUE BOAT

Arun is in big trouble.

The water is pulling him farther and farther away from shore. He tries to swim, but the waves are too strong. Every time he reaches for something to grab, it is either too small or zips past too fast.

Then he sees it – a fishing boat, flipped upside down, heading his way. It is blue. It looks just like the one their new friends had shown them on the beach.

Arun stretches out his arm. Too slippery! The boat slides right past him.

But wait – the nets are trailing behind!

With all his strength, Arun grabs a knot in the netting and hauls himself towards the boat. His feet tangle in the ropes, which helps him stay afloat. For the first time since being pulled out of the hotel, he has something solid to hold onto.

He hangs there, gasping. His legs dangle in the cold sea, and his arms ache from holding on. The boat starts drifting out to sea again, and panic rises in Arun's chest.

I can't float out here forever!

Just as he is about to let go, the boat jerks to a stop. It has hit something underwater – maybe debris or a tree. Either way, it isn't moving.

Arun rests his cheek against the cold wooden hull. He doesn't know how long he's been in the water. He doesn't care. For now, he is safe. Kind of.

He talks to himself quietly, trying to stay calm.

'I wish Sunil was here,' he mumbles.

Then, after a second, he says, 'No ... I'm glad he's not. This place is too scary.'

The cold water is messing with his brain. His teeth are chattering, and he feels like crying, but the tears won't come.

Then he sees something floating nearby.

A person. Face down.

Arun's heart stops.

He whispers a prayer – for the stranger, for himself, for everyone.

And then – like a switch has flipped – the boat lurches again. The current has yanked it loose.

Arun knows it's time.

Now or never.

He lets go and kicks hard. The waves suck at him like sticky hands trying to drag him under. He paddles weakly – more floating than swimming – but he keeps moving.

Then, in the distance, he hears voices.

'Hey! Over here!'

He squints and sees a house – two stories tall, still standing. People are on the balcony, waving and shouting.

'I'm here!' Arun yells. 'HELP!'

But the house is far. The current is strong. Arun kicks harder. But the voices get fainter. He isn't getting any closer.

'No, no, no!' he cries.

He rolls onto his back, trying to float and save energy. His arms are done. He can barely move.

The house fades behind him.

He shouts in anger and fear. 'Help me! PLEASE!'

Then the worst thing happens.

Crash.

He turns his head in time to see the house fall apart – its walls tumble into the water.

He thinks he hears people scream.

Then – nothing but waves.

6
THE IMPORTANCE OF TREES

Mr Soni clings to the broken seawall like his life depends on it – because it does.

Every muscle in his body is aching. But he won't stop. He can't. Arun is out there somewhere. He has to find him.

Despite Mrs Soni's protests, he has climbed out of the broken window, breaking off the jagged shards of glass as best he could. He had, of course, tried the door first, but the weight of the water held it shut fast. His head is bleeding, but in the mayhem he cannot remember hurting it.

Let go of the wall, he tells himself. You have to try.

He pushes off, swimming as best as he can. The current is still strong, but not as wild as before. Around him float walls, pieces of rooftops, chairs, even a refrigerator.

He keeps going.

Then – up ahead – palm trees! Three of them, still rooted in the ground.

He reaches out and grabs one trunk, then wraps his arms and legs around it like a koala bear. Another tree blocks the current. For the first time, he has a break.

Mr Soni loves trees. Always has. As a kid, he climbed them, planted them, built things with wood. Today, trees have just saved his life.

He rests a moment, then spots something in the distance.

A blue boat, floating upside down.

Could it be the same one the kids saw earlier? he wonders. But it's already too far to reach.

He knows he can't stop. Arun is still out there – somewhere. Maybe clinging to a boat. Maybe not.

Mr Soni forces his numb limbs to move again. His head still bleeds, and he is freezing, but he presses on.

In the distance, standing strong through the chaos, is the temple of Mahabalipuram. Something about it gives him hope.

Hold on, Arun. I'm coming.

7

VIEW FROM THE VERANDA

Back at the hotel, the water inside the room has started to drain away, slowly.

Mrs Soni holds Tara's hand in one of hers and Sunil's in the other as they carefully step across the wet floor. The water is still up to their knees, and they can't see what they are stepping on. Broken glass, floating furniture, tangled sheets – it's all hidden below.

'Where is everyone?' Sunil asks, peering through the smashed window. 'Why does it feel like we're the only ones left?'

Mrs Soni's heart is pounding, but she tries to keep calm for the kids. Tara is crying softly, and Sunil is doing his best to stay brave, but his lip keeps quivering.

The sky outside is blue. The sun is shining. It looks like a perfect beach day ... but it isn't. The ocean has taken over everything.

Mrs Soni tries the hotel room door again. Still jammed. She grabs a handbag, smashes out the rest of the broken window glass, and throws a bedsheet across the jagged sill like a makeshift curtain.

'Don't go, Mommy!' Tara cries.

'I'm not going far, sweetheart,' she says, giving her daughter a kiss. 'I'll lift you both out.'

She pulls Tara through the window first, then helps Sunil climb out. Now they are standing on the veranda – a narrow ledge just outside the hotel room. From here, they can see everything.

And what they see makes their stomachs twist.

The beach is gone. The whole area is underwater. Bits of houses float by – walls, chairs, mattresses, toys. Boats bob in the current like broken toys. Worst of all, they see people.

Some are swimming. Others aren't moving at all.

Tara buries her face in her mother's shirt.

'Where's Papa?' she whispers.

'And Arun?' Sunil asks.

Mrs Soni doesn't answer. She doesn't know. She holds them tighter and stares at the swirling mess that used to be their happy vacation.

Then – splash!

'TARA!' Sunil screams.

She'd slipped off the veranda!

Sunil jumps in without a second thought. He grabs her just as she starts to sink. Her arms are flailing, her mouth full of seawater.

Mrs Soni doesn't hesitate. She grabs the bedsheet still hanging from the window and tosses one end towards them, holding the other tightly.

'Grab it!' she shouts.

Sunil kicks and pulls. One arm holds Tara, the other grabs the sheet.

Mrs Soni hauls them back with all her strength.

They climb back onto the ledge, dripping and coughing. Mrs Soni bursts into tears.

'Don't cry, Mommy,' Tara says, her voice shaking. 'Sunil saved me.'

Mrs Soni hugs them both like she'll never let go.

Then they look out again – and wish they hadn't.

There are even more bodies floating by now. Too many.

Tara starts whimpering again. 'Why ... why are there so many people ...?'

Mrs Soni tries to shield her eyes, but it is impossible. There is no escape from what they are seeing.

Sunil grits his teeth. 'Papa will find Arun. I know he will.'

Mrs Soni nods and hugs them tighter. She keeps whispering the same promise over and over:

'I'll keep them safe. I'll keep them safe.'

Seagulls fly overhead, circling, looking for a place to land. There isn't one.

Then Tara points. 'Look!'

In the distance, the temple of Mahabalipuram still stands strong.

It gives them hope.

8
RESCUE

Just when Arun thinks he can't go another stroke, he sees it.

The rocky point near the temple.

Solid land.

He pushes through the freezing water with everything he has left. His arms are noodles, his legs barely move – but he keeps going.

Finally, he grabs onto a rock. He slips. Tries again. This time, his hands hold.

'Rocks,' he mutters. 'I love rocks.'

But he can't climb up. His muscles are shaking, his fingers numb. He is slipping – again!

Then –

A hand.

A strong hand.

It grabs his arm and doesn't let go.

He tries to look up, but the sun is too bright and everything is blurry.

He is dragged out of the water and up over the rocks. His body hurts all over. He is dizzy, soaked and barely breathing.

But then – he hears a voice.

'Arun. Arun! Oh, my son.'

It is his dad.

Mr Soni wraps his arms around Arun and holds him tight. Arun starts to cry – big, heavy sobs that shake his whole body. All the fear, pain and shock come rushing out.

His father notices the blood on Arun's side. Without a word, he tears off his own shirt and presses it against the wound.

'I've got you, son,' he whispers. 'I've got you.'

Arun winces in pain, then points weakly at his dad's gashed forehead.

They are both a mess. But they are alive. And they are together.

The temple stands above them like a guardian. Arun rests against one of the stone lions and feels ... safe.

'I didn't give up,' he whispers.

9

REUNION AND RECOVERY

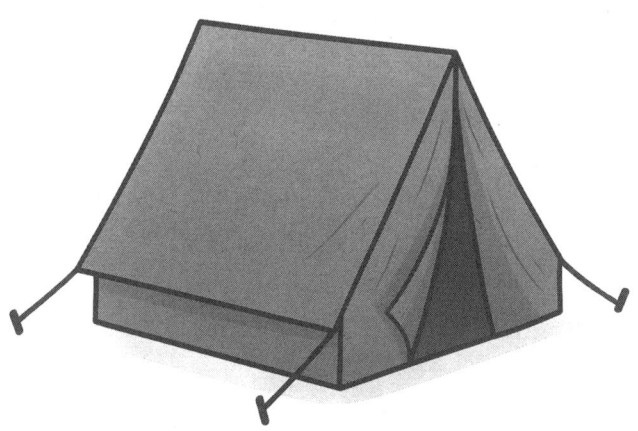

The next thing Arun knows, someone is shouting his name.

'Arun! Oh, Arun!'

He opens his eyes to see Tara's tear-streaked face and Sunil grinning with relief. His mom is hugging him tight, and his dad has one hand still on his bandaged side.

Everyone is crying and laughing all at once.

Later, at the local hospital, Arun gets seven stitches. His dad gets six.

'Ha! I beat you, Papa!' Arun jokes, managing a weak smile.

They laugh – not because anything is funny, but because it means things are starting to feel normal again. Just a little.

But nothing is really normal.

The hospital is full of people. Some are bandaged. Some are crying. Some are quiet and still – too still.

Tara looks around, clutching her mom's hand.

'I don't understand,' she whispers. 'I don't understand.'

Mr and Mrs Soni hug her close, but they don't have answers. No one does.

The hospital is overwhelmed. There are people on beds, on the floor, even in the courtyard. Doctors and nurses rush around, doing everything they can. Outside, families wait, hoping for news of their family members.

Tara notices that most of the people are locals – fishermen, shopkeepers, small children.

There are also tourists, like them. Some even look like they are from other countries.

'But what about our friends?' Tara asks suddenly. 'The boys from the fishing village?'

'And the rickshaw driver?' Sunil adds.

Mr Soni's face grows serious. 'Sometimes, the poorest people are the ones hurt the worst in disasters. Their homes are weaker. They live closer to danger. They don't have the same resources to escape or recover.'

Tara's eyes fill with tears.

'They were just boys,' she says. 'They didn't do anything wrong.'

'No one did,' Arun says quietly. 'It's not fair.'

The children search around the hospital. But there are so many people – hundreds – and it is impossible to find anyone in the chaos.

They never see the boys again.

They never find the rickshaw-wala either.

Later, the family huddles together and listen to a radio broadcast. That's when they begin to understand what had really happened.

A tsunami. One of the biggest and deadliest in history.

The wave had smashed into Indonesia, then Sri Lanka and the east coast of India – including Tamil Nadu, where they were. It kept going, even wrapping around to hit Kerala and distant places like the Maldives and the east coast of Africa.

The numbers are terrifying. Thousands dead. Many more missing.

In India alone, over 10,000 people have died. Most are from poor fishing villages like the one near their hotel.

The radio says that some fishermen had gone out to sea early in the morning and survived, while their families at home were swept away. In some places, the water had reached a full kilometre inland.

Sunil clenches his fists.

'It's not just water that has now receded,' he says. 'It's everything – homes, families, schools, memories – all gone.'

The reporters say Tamil Nadu has been hit the hardest in India. Whole villages have disappeared along with the roads that connect them – all gone.

Even cell towers and power lines have been destroyed, making communication nearly impossible.

'But what happens to all those people?' Tara asks. 'Where will they go?'

Her father answers gently, 'The government and military are trying to help. They're rescuing people, giving food and clean water. But it'll take a long time. And some things no one can fix.'

The Indian military had arrived quickly, setting up shelters, distributing supplies and clearing roads. NGOs – non-governmental organizations – have also come to help.

But it is overwhelming.

The kids see it first-hand. People building shelters from scraps of wood and plastic. Children wandering barefoot. Smoke rising from cooking fires made on the roadside.

And yet, through it all, they see people helping each other – sharing food, lifting spirits and carrying the injured.

Even in the darkest time, there is still kindness.

10
LET'S GO HOME

Communication is still a mess. Phones barely work. The lines are jammed, and towers near the coast have been destroyed. Messages get through slowly, if at all.

It isn't until days later that the Sonis finally leave the hospital and return to their hotel to gather what little they have left.

Tara stands at the spot where the lawn had once been. The flowers are gone. The seawall is broken. Their Christmas tree is just a soggy mess.

'I want to go home,' she whispers.

Everyone agrees.

But getting out isn't easy. Roads are blocked, and vehicles are hard to find. Everyone is trying to leave or trying to reach missing family.

Finally, Mr Soni finds a taxi.

The drive to Chennai is long and quiet. Along the road, they see families sitting under trees with makeshift shelters built from broken boards and plastic sheets. Some just sit and stare at the ocean. Others work, trying to fix nets or carry buckets of water.

'But why don't they leave?' Tara asks. 'Like we are doing?'

Sunil answers gently, 'Because they can't, Tara. Their homes are gone. Their money is gone. They don't have anywhere else to go.'

'It's not fair,' she says, shaking her head. 'Not at all.'

The family doesn't have an answer for that.

As they drive, they see tents being put up by aid workers and schools turned into shelters. People are doing their best to help.

The world has changed in just one day.

But the Sonis haven't just survived a tsunami; they have seen what it means to be strong, to be kind and to keep going, even when everything feels lost.

And now, finally, they are going home.

POSTSCRIPT

A REPORT ON TSUNAMIS

Back in Sikkim, Sunil wants to find out more about tsunamis and decides to write a report on it. He goes to the library, and his parents also help him contact people who know about the subject. This is what he finds.

Tsunamis are a natural force of nature. They are not uncommon, but the sheer size of the tsunami that hit Mahabalipuram is very rare. This tsunami actually originated thousands of miles away from Mahabalipuram. First, there were rumblings deep underground near the island of Sumatra in Indonesia. These rumblings continued throughout the day and during the night while Indians slept.

I Witnessed: The Indian Ocean Tsunami

Early in the morning on 26 December 2004, far underneath the ocean surface, the earth slipped. Huge plates of rock on the seabed strained against each other, shifted and shuddered. The ground began to shake and a fault line appeared in the floor of the Indian Ocean. It quickly spread, growing in scope and scale into a massive earthquake which lasted for ten minutes, with aftershocks.

Because the earthquake struck offshore, its centre (what is known as an epicentre) was not in human habitation, and, therefore, the quake itself did not cause significant damage to buildings and people in Indonesia. When an earthquake's epicentre is close to cities and towns, the immediate destruction can be devastating. Buildings collapse, roads break, fire breaks out and many lives are lost.

This was not the case with what came to be known as the Sumatra–Andaman earthquake. The initial quake was felt on land, but caused

UNDERWATER EARTHQUAKE

little damage. The damage, though, was to come. It would become one of the most destructive and devastating natural disasters in the history of the world.

The waves caused by the disruption underwater quickly grew. They started 100 kilometres away from the coast of Indonesia, but moved at an incredible speed, reaching the shore within minutes. Most people were simply unaware of the approaching danger as they moved about their morning's tasks or began to slowly wake up to the day.

One warning sign of an approaching tsunami is receding water. The huge wave is often preceded by a displacement of water along the shoreline. If this happens, people should immediately move to higher ground.

As the waves arrived at Indonesia's shoreline, they grew in height and ferocity, joining together into a massive wall of water, at times reaching 30 metres in height. That's roughly the height

of a ten-storey building! It is this wall of water that is known as a tsunami. The tsunami struck the island of Sumatra with fury, ripping through buildings and trees, and tearing apart lives. The tsunami also began moving across the Indian Ocean towards Thailand, Sri Lanka and India. This was the wave that eventually hit Mahabalipuram.

In India, the tsunami smashed into the islands of Andaman and Nicobar and the eastern coast, from Andhra Pradesh to Tamil Nadu. It wrapped around India's southern coast and crashed into the other side of the subcontinent in the state of Kerala. Many of these places had large numbers of fishing villages, such as in Mahabalipuram. These communities were especially vulnerable. Their dwellings were usually *kuccha*, often made from the flotsam and jetsam found along the beach.

The force of the tsunami was so enormous that once it had struck India's two coastlines

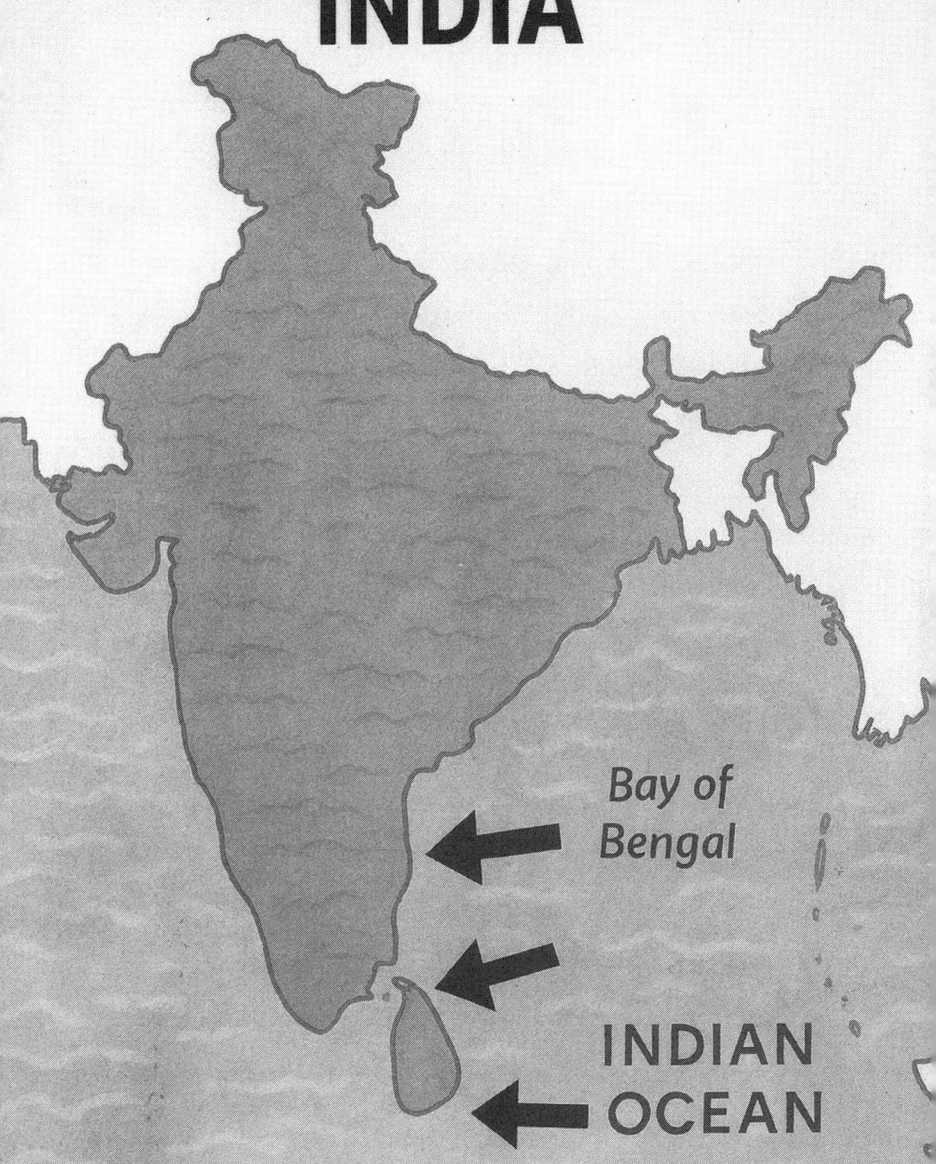

and ravaged Sri Lanka, it continued on to the Maldives, causing death and destruction there on the main island as well as among the Maldives's many resorts. Lakshadweep Islands, just to the north of the Maldives, was largely spared. But the monster wave continued across the Indian Ocean and crashed into the east coast of Africa with the coastal villages in Somalia, 4,500 kilometres away from the earthquake's epicentre.

Communities in the Seychelles, Kenya, Tanzania and even South Africa were impacted by the tsunami. Though the wave's power had largely dissipated by the time it reached Africa's southern coast, there were still unusually large swells that crashed into the continent in several places.

All of this took place in seven hours – from the time the earthquake struck until the wave reached the African continent. Hundreds of thousands of people died that morning, with

the majority near the earthquake's epicentre in Indonesia. Over 2,30,000 people lost their lives across Indonesia, Thailand, Sri Lanka and India. In India, over 10,000 people were killed, and over 5,000 were reported missing. Some of the missing were eventually found but many were never found and presumed to be swept away. Tamil Nadu was the hardest hit of all the Indian states.

OTHER BOOKS IN THE SERIES

3 December 1984, Bhopal.

Vikram is sneaking back home after a night out with his friends when the sirens at the nearby gas factory start to wail. A strange, choking smell fills the air. Within minutes, the streets are a nightmare – people and animals lying on the ground, eyes red, mouths foaming. The stench of rotten cabbages hangs everywhere.

Terrified, Vikram wakes his little brother up. Together, they run into the dark night, trying to escape the invisible poison swirling through their city. But where can they go? And how far will they get before it's too late?

26 January 2001, Chobari.

Seema was sipping tea. Her little sister, Padma, was playing with her dolls. Suddenly, the ground began to shake. At first, it was just a tremor. Then the floor rippled like waves. Walls cracked. Roofs collapsed. The sisters ran – but the world was falling apart.

Now they're trapped under the rubble, dust in their lungs, fear in their hearts. Seema knows she has to stay calm and find a way out before the next tremor hits. Can she save Padma and herself before it's too late?